Alligators, Alligators

by Eve Bunting

Illustrated by Diane Ewen

Clarion Books ★ An Imprint of HarperCollinsPublishers

Clarion Books is an imprint of HarperCollins Publishers.

Alligators, Alligators
Text copyright © 2023 by Eve Bunting
Illustrations copyright © 2023 by Diane Ewen

ISBN 978-1-32-884626-6

The artist used Photoshop to create the digital illustrations for this book.
Typography by Stephanie Hays
23 24 25 26 27 RTLO 10 9 8 7 6 5 4 3 2 1

First Edition

For all my great-grandchildren, with love.
—E.B.

For S.E. Dance like an alligator.
—D.E.

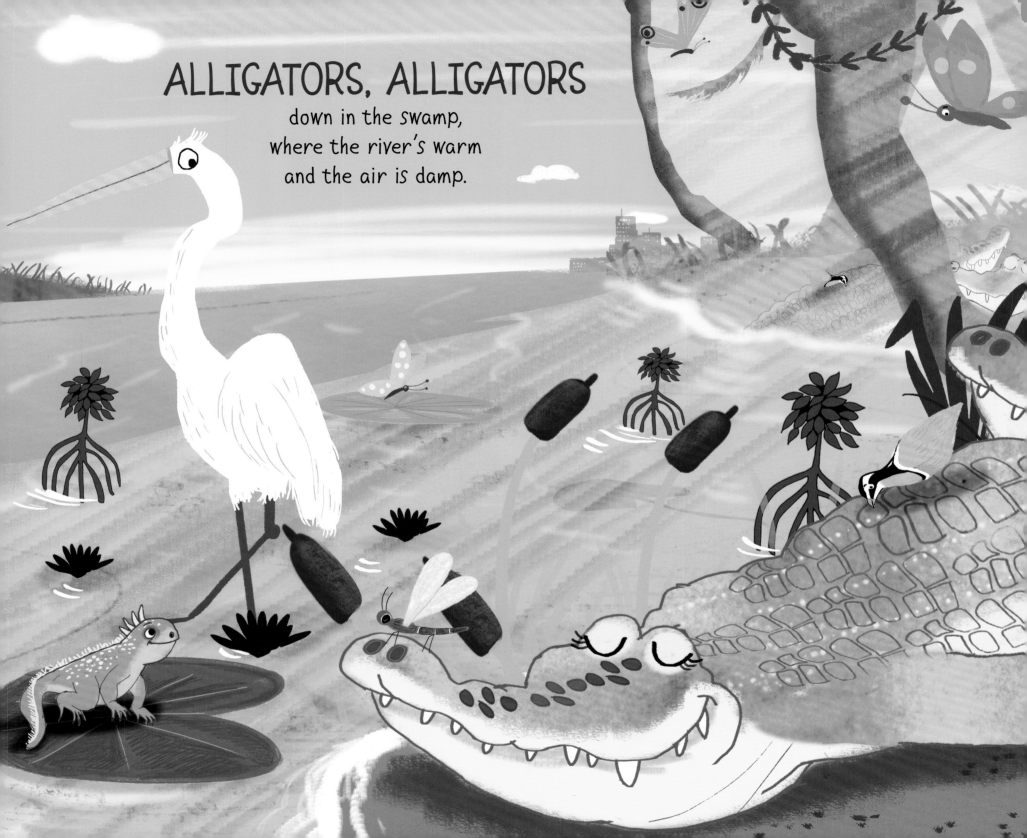

ALLIGATORS, ALLIGATORS
down in the swamp,
where the river's warm
and the air is damp.

Alligators lying in
riverbank mud,
sunshine warming their
cold, cold blood.

There's a sound upriver coming their way.
They don't get to hear it every day.

Laughter and chatter
and a whistle blast.
The big tourist boat
is coming at last.

The captain stands. The big boat stops. There's a rattle of sound as the anchor drops. He points to a boy. "This here is Jim. He's ten years old, and I'm proud of him.

"He has a talent, and soon you will see how creatures respond to his melody."

Jim fingers his flute and the music rises, music that nobody recognizes.

Not one of the tourists makes a sound
as the gators slide in and swim slowly around.

But there is a man in a shiny, black suit
who is watching only the boy and his flute.

The gators sway and sashay and one pirouettes.
They're cold-blooded killers acting like pets.

Are they dancing the stories their ancestors told
of centuries past, when the new world was old?

Jim quiets his music and the tourists can hear another big boat coming noisily near.

He puts down his flute and goes back to his chair.
A breath of his music still hangs in the air.

The gators glide over to where they had lain,
to rest in the mud and be gators again.

The anchor is raised. Roscoe's boat pulls away.
But first, the captain has something to say.

"Maybe you've heard that these gators were trained,
so that tourists like you would be well entertained.

You can't train a gator. That rumor's not true.
The gator would eat you before you were through.

"The gift of this music
belongs to my Jim.

Animals gather
to listen to him.

He loves all
earth's creatures,
the big and the small.

Be they savage or tame,
he plays for them all.

"My son doesn't brag about what he can do, but he has agreed that I can tell you.
I've seen wild coyotes slink up close to Jim, sit in a circle, and listen to him."

The man in the suit has come up with a plan.
It's been on his mind since the music began.

He'll steal Jim's flute. Fly to some distant land.
Wild beasts will come at the flute's command.

Poachers and hunters will pay him a lot
for the creatures he'll bring, endangered or not.

The boat trip has ended, the tourists stream down,
they're leaving the dock now and heading for town.

But the man in the suit has remained in his place.
Now he gets to his feet with a smile on his face.

He walks up to Jim
in the friendliest way,
as if he has something
important to say.

No one is watching, there's no one around.
He snatches the flute and jumps down to the ground.

Jim shouts, "Hey, come back here!" But to his dismay,
the man jumps in a car and drives quickly away.

The man in the suit is as proud as can be.
He took what he wanted and got away free.

The river is close and he's ready to play.
Everything's fine. This is his lucky day!

The music he plays
doesn't sound very good,
but the gators arrive.
He was certain they would.

Are these the same gators
that started to dance
when Jim played this flute?
He thinks there's a chance.

The gators aren't dancing. So why are they here?
He is suddenly filled with a terrible fear.

Then comes a splash and a slithery thud as one of the gators crawls out through the mud.

The man screws his eyes shut and scrunches up tight, awaiting the pain of that terrible bite.

But when nothing happens, he falls to the ground,
half opens his eyes, and peers all around.

The gators are gone. The flute is gone too.
He looks at the river and thinks it all through.

They came for the flute he had stolen from Jim.
They wanted the flute, but they didn't want him.

Evening arrives. It's past six o'clock.
Roscoe and Jim are still on the dock,
cleaning the boat, shining it bright,
making it safe for the rest of the night.

The river is peaceful, sleepy and dark,
reflecting the lights of the riverside park.

Jim sees the gators. He stands up to check,
and one drops the flute so it rolls on the deck.

He picks up the flute
and commences to play.
The gators are waiting,
they're starting to sway.

They're moving together, as if in a trance.
Slowly and softly, they're starting to dance.

So much for the man in the shiny, black suit who'd thought that Jim's power belonged to his flute.

The flute wasn't magic. The flute didn't do it. The power was Jim's love that came whispering through it.

Roscoe walks home
with his arm round his son.
The day has been tiring,
but now it is done.

Strangers who notice them think it is cute
that the young boy is walking and playing his flute,

then halt, amazed to see at his feet

two bobcats there dancing a jig in the street.